MW01242359

This Book Belongs to:

____

Made in the USA
Middletown, DE
21 December 2021

56859063R00068